SHLAND

D0398685

Who's on First?

MARK GELLER

JACKSON COUNTY LIBRARY SYSTEM
MEDFORD, OREGON 97501

A Charlotte Zolotow Book
An Imprint of HarperCollins*Publishers*

The poem on pages 8–9 and on page 58, "An Immortality," is from *Personae* by Ezra Pound. Copyright © 1976 by the Ezra Pound Literary Property Trust. Reprinted by permission of New Directions Publishing Corporation.

Who's on First?
Copyright © 1992 by Mark Geller
All rights reserved. No part of this book may be used or reproduced in any manner whatsoever without written permission except in the case of brief quotations embodied in critical articles and reviews. Printed in the United States of America. For information address HarperCollins Children's Books, a division of HarperCollins Publishers, 10 East 53rd Street, New York, NY 10022.
Typography by Daniel C. O'Leary
1 2 3 4 5 6 7 8 9 10
First Edition

Library of Congress Cataloging-in-Publication Data
Geller, Mark.
  Who's on first? / by Mark Geller.
    p.   cm.
  "A Charlotte Zolotow book."
  Summary: When fourteen-year-old Alex involves himself in his older sister's love life, he almost ruins her chance at true happiness.
  ISBN 0-06-021084-2. — ISBN 0-06-021085-0 (lib. bdg.)
  [1. Brothers and sisters—Fiction.]   I. Title.
PZ7.G279Wi   1992   91-46184
[Fic]—dc20   CIP
                                                                  AC

For Jesse and for Norman

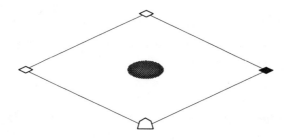

MY MOTHER and her sister Ida were in the living room of our apartment. Ida had come to visit. I was in my room, about to leave for baseball practice, lying on my bed, listening to their conversation.

It was July. Ida's daughter Amanda's wedding was less than three weeks away. Ida said that Amanda had let her read the vows that she and her fiancé, Joel, had written.

"They're beautiful," Ida said.

"That's nice," my mother said.

"You must see Amanda in her gown. She's stunning."

"I'm sure she is."

"Joel is a delicious boy. He's mad about Amanda. It seems not so long ago that my Amanda and your Carol were small children, doesn't it?"

"It does."

"They were such good playmates. Amanda still speaks fondly of Carol. Carol will be seated at a table with the cousins. I hope she's not uncomfortable that the others have escorts."

"Carol doesn't seem uncomfortable about that at all," my mother said.

"I'm glad," Ida said. "Amanda and Joel have been shopping for a bedroom set. Joel has impeccable taste."

◆　　◆　　◆

I WALKED to practice with Alan Paine. I didn't have much to say. Paine asked if something was on my mind.

"My cousin Amanda is getting married," I said. "My sister has no escort. She might be uncomfortable about it. My mother doesn't think so, but I do."

Paine asked why my sister didn't get herself an escort if she was uncomfortable without one, and I said that it wasn't that easy. I said that my sister had no boyfriend and didn't even have an active social life.

Paine said that that was too bad. I said I wished I could do something for her. Paine said that maybe I could introduce her to someone.

"Who?" I said.

"Don't you know anyone?"

"No. Amanda probably had a couple hundred boyfriends. She's having the wedding of the century. My uncle made a fortune in the restaurant supplies business. My aunt isn't sparing any expense."

MY MOTHER was preparing dinner when I got home.

"Look at your clothes," she said.

"I dove for a ground ball. Where's Ida?"

"Ida left a long time ago. Those are your good jeans."

I sat at the kitchen table.

"Ma."

"What?"

"Do I have to go to the wedding?"

"What did you say?" my mother said, turning to me from the cabinet, where she was looking for something.

"I don't like weddings," I said.

"That's too bad about you," my mother said.

"I'm not going to dance."

"That's your prerogative."

"I'm too old for the children's table."

"Fourteen isn't too old."

"What if I have to sit next to cousin Philip?"

"You'll be polite and friendly if you know what's good for you."

"That's what I mean about weddings. You have to get dressed up and sit with people you don't like and be friendly and polite to them. I don't see why you're making me go. Didn't Ida invite a couple of thousand guests? No one would miss me."

◆　◆　◆

I WENT to see my sister in her room. She was at her desk writing. I sat on her bed.

She's an English teacher at Adlai Stevenson Junior High School in Manhattan. She takes graduate courses at night and in the summer at Queens College.

She's tall and has a narrow face like my father's. She's ten years older than I am.

"Are you writing a paper?" I said.

"Yes," she said, not stopping.

"What's it about?"

"Robert Graves."

"Who?"

"Robert Graves. He's an author. He wrote *I, Claudius*."

"Is it good?"

"Yes, it's good," my sister said. She put down her pencil and faced me. "What do you want, Alex?"

"Nothing."

"Did you come to visit?"

"Yes."

"Why?"

"We haven't talked in a while."

"We talk all the time, Alex."

"We don't have real conversations, though."

She squinted her eyes at me, then crossed her legs and folded her arms in front of her.

"What would you like to discuss, then, Alex?"

"What would you like to discuss?"

"You initiated the discussion, Alex. You should choose the subject."

"We had practice today. The coach was giving me instructions on playing shortstop. His name is Willie. He's a great coach. He's a good baseball player, too. He's a technical writer. I don't even know what that is. He works for himself, so he has time to coach. He told us he enjoys it."

"What else should we discuss?"

6

"What do you think of capital punishment? I saw a television show on it."

"I'm against it."

"Most of the audience was for it."

"I'm not surprised."

"Do you think our largest cities are governable?"

"Did you watch a show about that, too?"

"We read an article about it for social studies last year. Did you get your hair cut?"

"Yes."

"It looks good. How come you don't wear that much makeup?"

"Why are you asking me that?"

"Ida was here today. She wears a lot of makeup."

"She does."

"I'm not crazy about her. She calls me 'dear.' She thinks Amanda should be queen of New York or something. Do you think Uncle Bob is glad he married her?"

"I don't have reason to think he isn't," my sister said, smiling.

"You look good without makeup," I said.

"Thank you."

"You have attractive brown eyes."

"Why, Alex. All these compliments."

"Do you remember that poem by Ezra Pound you made your class read last year? I was looking over your shoulder one day and read it."

"I remember."

"How did it go again?"

"Did you like it so much?"

"Yes."

"Would you like me to read it to you?"

"If you want."

She reached for a book from the shelf above her desk, found the right page and began to read.

Sing we for love and idleness,
Naught else is worth the having.

Though I have been in many a land,
There is naught else in living.

And I would rather have my sweet,
Though rose leaves die of grieving,

Than do high deeds in Hungary
To pass all men's believing.

"That is pretty, isn't it?" my sister said, closing the book.

"What does it mean?" I said.

"I think it means that nothing in the world is so good and important and precious as love."

"Do you believe that?" I said.

"Yes, I believe that," my sister said.

I stared at her, thinking what a good person she was and how glad I was that she was my sister. Then I apologized for keeping her from her work and left the room.

◆　　◆　　◆

PAINE CALLED that night.

"I thought of someone," he said.

"For what?"

"I thought of someone to meet your sister."

"What do you mean?"

"You said you wanted your sister to meet someone. I thought of someone."

"Who?"

"My cousin Leon. He's an investment analyst. He got out of college a few years ago. He's already pretty successful. He drives a Porsche. He wants to meet someone himself."

"How do you know?"

"My mother told me."

"Did you tell your mother what I told you about my sister?"

"I'll tell my mother it's all right for my cousin to call your sister."

"That was supposed to be confidential, Paine."

"Your sister can say no if she doesn't want to meet him. No one's forcing her. He's not going to come to your door. What do you say? Say it's all right so my mother can call my aunt and tell her to tell my cousin to call your sister."

♦　　♦　　♦

I SAID all right. But I wasn't sure it was. I worried about it awhile, then called my mother to my room and told her what I had done.

I was sitting up on the bed. She sat on the bed near me.

I asked if I had done something wrong and if she thought my sister would be upset. I said I could call Paine to say I had changed my mind.

She said I hadn't done anything wrong, though it was certainly bold of me. She asked if it was Paine's idea for his cousin to call my sister, and I told her what I had told Paine on the way to practice.

She asked if I was really concerned. I said I was because my sister was quiet and reserved and what if she never had a boyfriend and never got married and always was lonely?

11

My mother said she was surprised at me. She thought I knew that not having a boyfriend or husband didn't mean being lonely and unhappy. She said that women without boyfriends and husbands led full and rich lives.

She asked if my sister seemed unhappy and I said she didn't. She asked if my sister seemed lonely and I said she didn't.

She said that my sister was young. She had friends. She was a joy to us all. She'd probably have a boyfriend someday. She'd probably get married. Whether she did or didn't, she'd have a good life.

Then she tapped my hand and smiled. She said I was sweet to worry. It was sweet even if it was needless.

◆　　◆　　◆

PAINE'S COUSIN called my sister the next day while I was at the schoolyard playing basketball. When I got home, she followed me to my room. I suspected that Paine's cousin had called so I did my best to act casual.

"What's up?" I said.

"Someone called me this morning."

"Yeah. Who?"

"Leon Miller."

"Who's he?" I said, sticking my basketball into the closet.

"He said that Alan Paine is his cousin."

"Oh, yeah. That's right."

"He asked me to go out with him."

"That's nice. Have you had lunch? I'm hungry."

"You can explain all this, can't you, Alex?"

"Let's see. I know. Paine and I were talking on the way to practice yesterday and he mentioned that he had this cousin. He was an investment counselor or something and he wanted to meet someone."

"Go on."

"Paine said, 'What about your sister?' And I said, 'What about her?' And he asked if you'd mind if he gave his cousin your name so he could call you. I gave it some thought and said I didn't think you'd mind because you could always say no if you didn't want to go out with him and he wasn't going to come to your door. You didn't mind him calling, did you?"

"Not really."

"How did he seem?"

"He seemed all right."

"What are you going to do?"

"What am I going to do about what?"

"Are you going to go out with him? I'm not trying to invade your privacy."

"Yes. I told him that I 'd go out with him."

"Maybe he'll be nice," I said. "You can never tell. I mean, there's nothing to lose."

◆　　◆　　◆

SATURDAY AROUND seven o'clock Paine's cousin came to take my sister on their date. I opened the door for him and we said hello and my parents came from the living room to say hello.

My mother said that my sister would be ready in a minute. Paine's cousin said he had heard I was on his cousin's baseball team and asked if I was a Yankee fan.

"Is he ever," my mother said.

"What do you think of Alvaro Espinoza?" Paine's cousin asked.

"He's one of my favorite players," I said.

"He's a friend of mine," Paine's cousin said.

"He is?" I said.

"I'm helping him with his investments. He's going to introduce me to some of the other Yankees. Maybe I'll ask him for tickets to take you and my cousin to a game."

"You will?"

"Why not? I haven't been to a game in a while myself. I'll see if Alvaro can get us into the club-house."

My sister came from her room and she and Paine's cousin said hello to each other. My father wished them a good time as they left. My mother said, when the door closed behind them, that he seemed like a nice boy.

◆　　◆　　◆

I RUSHED to my room and called Paine. I was pretty excited. I asked why he hadn't told me that his cousin knew Alvaro Espinoza.

"No reason," he said.

"Didn't you think I'd be interested?" I said.

"Yeah."

"He might ask Alvaro for tickets to take you and me to a game. We might get into the clubhouse."

"He told me that last year," Paine said.

"What do you mean he told you that last year? Why didn't he take you, then?"

"I don't know."

"Didn't you ask him?"

"Yeah. He said he hadn't seen much of Alvaro lately. My father said—"

"What did your father say?"

"He said I shouldn't hold my breath."

16

"Why did he say that?"

"I don't know."

"Is your cousin unreliable or something?"

"Maybe."

"Oh, man, Paine. He really knows Alvaro Espinoza, doesn't he?"

"Yeah, he knows him. My father—"

"What, Paine?"

"Nothing."

"What, Paine?"

"My father said he probably knows him but he might not know him that well. He might've only met him once."

"Your cousin is a liar."

"No, he isn't."

"You said yourself he lied."

"He exaggerated."

"What's the difference?"

"There's a big difference."

"Not as far as I'm concerned. You're swell. You know that, Paine? You have my sister dating a pathological liar."

17

MY SISTER came home late when my parents were sleeping. I waited a minute and went to her room.

"Hi," I said from the doorway.

She turned—she was at the bureau taking off her earrings—and asked what I was doing up.

"I couldn't sleep," I said. "How did it go?"

"It went all right," she said.

"What did you do?"

"We went to a movie and a diner."

"Did you like him?"

"Yes."

"How come?"

"Why shouldn't I? He was pleasant."

"Did he tell you about any celebrities he knew?"

"No."

"Are you going to go out with him again?"

"Yes. I'm seeing him next Saturday. Please leave. I want to undress. Do you know what time it is?"

♦   ♦   ♦

WE HAD a game Wednesday and my sister came.
She'd been promising to come watch me play for a
long time.

Paine's cousin came, too. He'd called my sister
about something else the night before and she'd
told him about the game and he'd said that he
wouldn't mind seeing a game himself.

Both of them brought lounge chairs. They sat
together in foul territory behind first base and
seemed to be chatting all game long.

I took a walk to the water fountain while we
were up in the fifth inning. I met Paine's cousin
there and we walked back to the field together.

"Tough game," he said.

"Yeah," I said.

"Are you losing eleven to two? I lost track."

"Twelve to two," I said.

"Who's the fat kid playing second base?"

"Bloom."

"He's killing you. He made about six errors.

19

Your coach should get him out of the game."

"Willie wouldn't do that," I said.

"Oh, no? Why wouldn't he?"

"It would hurt Bloom's feelings."

"So what?"

"Willie doesn't care about winning. He wants us to learn about baseball and enjoy ourselves."

"That's well and good," Paine's cousin said. "I don't see it that way, though. The way I see it, if you're going to play at all, you might as well play to win.

"Did I tell you that I played second base in high school myself? Once this guy was rounding second headed for third. I tripped him. He fell and had to scramble back to second. He complained but the umpire hadn't seen it. That's what I mean about doing what it takes to win.

"Take this game. You guys aren't hitting. You only have four or five hits. Their pitcher is in a groove. You have to rattle him. Somebody should lay a bunt down the first-base line and run him over when he tries to field it.

"You know how else to rattle a pitcher? You look for something about him that he's probably sensitive about. Say he has big ears or something. You taunt him about it from the bench. Pretty soon he's not concentrating on the game anymore."

"Willie would never let us do that."

"Willie better let you try something. How are you supposed to enjoy yourselves losing twenty to two?"

◆　　◆　　◆

WE LOST nineteen to five. We congratulated the other team, and Willie told us that he was proud of us, and I brought him to meet my sister.

"Carol, this is Willie. Willie, this is Carol."

"Hello, Carol."

"Hello."

"Did you enjoy the game?" Willie asked.

"Yes."

"Alex is a good player."

"So he's been telling me."

They were staring at each other.

"He's improving all the time," Willie said.

"Oh, is there room for improvement?" my sister said.

"He told me that you're a teacher."

"I am."

"He said that you're a good teacher."

"He's not in a position to know. He told me that you're a writer."

"I am."

They were staring at each other again. Paine's cousin came from talking to Paine at the side to ask my sister if she wanted a ride home. My sister stared a second more at Willie, then turned to Paine's cousin and said all right.

Then she said, "Willie, do you know Leon? Leon, do you know Willie?"

"Hello," Willie said.

"Tough game," Paine's cousin said, then asked if I wanted a ride home, too. I said I'd rather walk. My sister told Willie it was nice meeting him and Willie said it was nice meeting her and she left with Paine's cousin.

♦   ♦   ♦

PAINE WALKED home with me. I told him what his cousin had said on the way from the water fountain. I said that he was a creep.

"Don't call my cousin a creep," Paine said.

"Why shouldn't I?" I said.

"I said so," Paine said.

"Are you denying he's a creep?" I said.

"Yeah, I'm denying it," Paine said.

"He's a jerk," I said.

"Don't call my cousin a jerk."

"He's a jerk, so I'll call him a jerk."

"Your sister doesn't think he's a jerk. She went out with him once and she's going to go out with him again. It looked like they were enjoying each other's company at the game, too."

"Oh, yeah?" I said.

"Oh, yeah," Paine said.

"My sister will come to her senses," I said. "Face it, Paine. Your cousin is a jerk. He's a creep and a jerk."

◆　　◆　　◆

MY SISTER and Paine's cousin had their second date. I prayed that it would be terrible and that she'd realize what a terrible person he was.

I wanted to stay awake to ask but fell asleep before she came home. Instead of going to the schoolyard in the morning I waited for her to wake up.

While she sat at the kitchen table in her bathrobe, talking to my mother standing by the stove, I poured myself a glass of milk and sat across from her. I tried not to be too obvious about what I wanted to know.

"Good morning," I said.

"Good morning," my sister said.

"How's the coffee?"

"The coffee is fine."

"You probably need it. You got home late."

"Yes, I did."

"What about some eggs?" my mother said.

"Fine," my sister said.

"You probably had a good time, then," I said.

"Why?" my sister said.

"You probably wouldn't have stayed out so late if you weren't having a good time."

"Not necessarily."

I grew hopeful.

"I'll scramble the eggs," my mother said.

"That's too bad," I said.

"What's too bad?" my sister said.

"It's too bad you didn't have a better time."

"Did I say I didn't have a good time?" my sister said after sipping her coffee.

"You said you didn't necessarily have a good time."

"No, I said that staying out late didn't necessarily mean that I had a good time. I didn't say that I didn't have a good time."

"Did you?"

"Did I what?"

"Did you have a good time?"

She said she had and my heart sank.

"You didn't change your opinion about Paine's cousin?" I said.

"Not really."

"Good. I mean, I know you liked him after the first date and everything. I'm glad that you still like him."

◆   ◆   ◆

TUESDAY my sister came to another game. She hadn't told me that she was coming. She arrived in the second inning, waved at me in the field and placed her chair not far from our bench.

"What are you doing here?" I asked when we came up to bat.

"I came to watch the game."

"Why?"

"I enjoyed the last game and needed a break from my work. You don't mind, do you?"

The next inning, when we were in the field, Willie walked over to my sister and talked to her.

"What were you and Willie discussing?" I asked when we got up.

"I don't remember."

"I saw you smile."

"I'm allowed to smile. Please, Alex. Go to your bench and let me watch the game."

Willie talked to my sister again when we were in the field during the fifth inning. When we were in the field during the sixth inning, my sister left. She waved at me on her way and said something to Willie, and he said something to her.

◆　　　◆　　　◆

MY SISTER left after dinner the next day and didn't come home until past midnight. I was awake in bed and heard the front door open.

"Shh. Everyone is sleeping," my sister said.

"I had a good time," a man's hushed voice said.

"I did, too," my sister said.

"We'll be seeing each other again before you know it," the man said.

"We will," my sister said.

"Good night," the man said.

"Good night," my sister said.

"Sleep tight," the man said.

The door closed and I heard my sister go to her room.

"It's not enough he sees her every Saturday," I thought. "Now he has to start seeing her on weekdays."

◆　　◆　　◆

WHEN I came home from the schoolyard the next afternoon, my mother grinned at me. I said, "What?" and she told me to guess and I told her I didn't want to guess.

She said it concerned the wedding. I said it was canceled and she said it wasn't that and I said Philip wasn't going to be there and she said it wasn't that either.

She said, with a bigger grin, that someone else was going to be at the wedding, too. I knew then what she was going to tell me. The thought of it had come to my mind once or twice and was so unpleasant that I had made it go away.

I told my mother that she didn't have to tell me. I knew that my sister had an escort to the wedding.

My mother asked how I knew, and before I answered, asked why I didn't look happier. I told her that I was never happier in my life and that I was going to my room and might not be hungry for dinner.

◆　　　◆　　　◆

WHEN MY sister came home, she spoke to my mother, then came to my room. I was on the floor looking at baseball cards. She asked if any were valuable and I shrugged.

She said, sitting on the bed, that she and I had something to discuss. She said she knew I'd rather someone else were escorting her to the wedding and that she understood.

"It's awkward for you, isn't it?" she said.

"No."

"It must be. You're not uninvolved. He's your—"

"I said it's not awkward."

"What is it, then, Alex? Why do you seem unhappy?"

I looked up from the cards.

"Do you want to know?" I said.

"Yes."

"I'll tell you. I don't like him."

"What do you mean?" my sister said.

"I mean what I said. I don't like him. He's not a nice person."

"How can you say that?"

"I'm saying it because it's true. I caught him in a lie."

"What kind of lie?"

"What's the difference? He's a liar. He's insensitive. He made fun of Bloom."

"I can't imagine—"

"He thinks cheating is all right. He said someone should run over the other team's pitcher and that we should taunt him to ruin his concentration. He bragged about cheating himself in high school.

"He's not a nice person. I know him now. He's not what he seems. I'm telling you he's not a nice person."

◆   ◆   ◆

MY SISTER stared at me, shook her head, and then left the room. She returned fifteen minutes later. I was still on the floor, telling myself that I'd said what I had to say.

"I called him," my sister said. "I hope you're satisfied. He won't be escorting me."

"Did you tell him what I said?"

"No."

"What, then?"

"I told him that I'd given it more thought and didn't want to subject him to our relatives. There's even some truth in that. I'd had reservations about having him escort me."

"What did he say?"

"He was disappointed. He tried to get me to change my mind. He nearly succeeded. I'm not at all sure I should've done this.

"I did it for you, Alex. I know, now that you've expressed yourself about him, how much you don't want him at the wedding. I don't want to spoil the evening for you.

"But I intend to keep seeing him, Alex. I want you to know that.

"We have a different opinion of him. The person you know is not the person I know. The person I know is sweet and kind.

"I'm fond of him, Alex. I'm growing more fond of him all the time."

◆　　◆　　◆

THE NEXT day was Amanda's wedding. The only good thing was that we'd be getting it over with.

I showered when my mother said it was my turn and got dressed. I shoved a transistor radio into my jacket pocket and joined everyone at the front door.

"Let me look at you. Your tie is askew," my mother said.

"Who cares?" I said.

"I do," she said, straightening it.

My sister was subdued. I knew she must be thinking of Paine's cousin. She was wearing a blue dress and lipstick and blusher and dangling earrings. I didn't tell her how nice she looked because I thought she'd think I was only saying it to make up for what happened with Paine's cousin.

"Change expressions, Alex," my mother said as we waited for the elevator. "We 're not going to a funeral."

◆　　◆　　◆

"HELLO. HELLO," Ida said, hurrying to greet us in the lobby at Maurice's Royal Manor. "I'm so glad that you're here."

She was wearing a red dress with sequins. It probably cost a few thousand dollars. She has a good figure for someone her age.

Bob came right behind her carrying a drink. He said, "Look what came with the breeze. What do you think of this place? I'm not saying what it's costing me. Don't let a chandelier fall on you."

"I love your dress," Ida told my mother.

"Thank you," my mother said.

"I love your dress, too, Carol," Ida said.

"Thank you," my sister said.

"What are you doing here?" Bob said.

"Me?" I said.

"I'm not looking at anyone else," Bob said.

"I was invited," I said.

"Why would I invite you? I don't even like you. I'll give you money for a cab home."

"Oh, Bob," Ida said.

"'Oh, Bob,'" he mimicked her and took a drink.

"The Nugents are here," Ida said, leaving us for them. "Hello, Earl. Hello, Miriam. Miriam, your dress is lovely."

◆　　◆　　◆

THE WEDDING ceremony was held in a room that said "Chapel" on the door. Someone told you to sit on a bench to the left or right depending on whether you were with the bride's party or groom's party.

My cousin Tina was a bridesmaid in a fluffy pink dress. She smiled at me on her way down the aisle. She's ten years old and crazy about me.

Bob escorted Amanda down the aisle. "She's a doll," a woman with a loud voice said.

I'd never seen so many flowers in one place. My mother whispered to my father that they were beautiful.

The ceremony was boring. The worst part was the vows that Amanda and Joel had written.

I glanced at my sister sitting on the other side of my parents from me. I thought that she must be thinking of Paine's cousin.

Amanda and Joel were pronounced man and wife. He gave her a long kiss and half the audience went "Aaaah."

◆   ◆   ◆

AFTER HORS D'OEUVRES in the Blue Room—I nearly gagged on liver pâté and my mother introduced me to her second cousin—dinner was served in the dining room. I took the seat I was assigned at the children's table and put the radio to my ear. Philip took the seat next to me.

"Something interesting?" he said. He's my age and a genius. He's supposed to start college after ninth grade or something.

"Yeah, something interesting."

"It's a baseball game, isn't it?"

"What makes you say that?"

"I do know a bit about you, cousin Alex, and, if the radio were louder, I could hear the score. You know my opinion of baseball, don't you?"

"Don't tell me."

"It's not only baseball to which I object. It's all professional sports. It seems to me the culture is hardly enriched—"

"There. I'm not listening anymore. Are you satisfied?" I said, returning the radio to my pocket.

"Hello, Alex."

It was Tina, sitting on the other side of me.

"Hi," I said.

"I'm glad we're next to each other."

"Yeah, I am, too."

"Are you going to dance later?"

"I doubt it," I said. "I'm not in the mood."

◆　　◆　　◆

THE LIGHTS got dim so Amanda and Joel could dance the first dance under a spotlight. Tina said that they looked beautiful together.

Philip asked if I'd read *Out of the Silent Planet* by C. S. Lewis and I said I'd missed it. Philip said it was both entertaining science fiction and a compelling defense of Christian theology and I said I'd have to give it a try.

The waiters served dinner. I had prime rib of beef with mashed potatoes and string beans.

Tina said her birthday was in a month. She said she was having boys to her party and asked if I wanted to come. I said I was usually pretty busy and that I'd have to see about it.

Ida visited our table. She'd been visiting all the tables. She asked if we'd all like to have such a beautiful wedding someday and Tina and a few other girls said they would.

Tina asked if I'd gotten in the mood to dance. I said that I hadn't.

I put the radio to my ear again. Philip said that I was guilty of a serious breach of etiquette—not that he had much patience with bourgeois etiquette himself.

I'd had enough. I left the table and the dining room and didn't stop until I was on the steps in front of Maurice's Royal Manor listening to the Yankee game with no one to bother me.

◆　　◆　　◆

I'D LISTENED to an inning when there was a tap on my shoulder. It was my sister. I shut the radio off and she sat beside me.

She said everyone wondered where I'd gone. I said I needed to be by myself awhile. She asked if that meant I wasn't enjoying Philip's company. I said I didn't understand half of what he said.

"You're not having the time of your life, then?" she said.

"No. Are you?" I said.

"Bob amuses me."

"He's drinking too much."

"Yes, he is. Ida amuses me in her way."

"She doesn't amuse me."

"No, Alex, I'm not having the time of my life either."

I stared at her staring at the fountain in front of us.

"I'm sorry," I said.

"Why?"

"You'd be having a better time if you had an escort."

"That depends on the escort."

"I did the right thing, didn't I? Didn't I have to tell you?"

"You did."

"I mean, I couldn't keep it from you. You're not upset with me, are you?"

"No."

"I wish I'd never told Paine to tell him it was all right to call you."

"Say that again," my sister said.

"Paine's ideas are never any good."

"Alex—"

"I'm surprised you liked him."

"Alex—"

"He doesn't seem like the kind of person you'd like."

"Oh, God, Alex," my sister said, and buried her face in her hands.

"I'm sorry I said that," I said. "Are you really so unhappy? I didn't know you cared so much about him. I'm sorry, Carol."

"Let's go inside," my sister said, taking her hands from her face. "We don't want to miss too much of the wedding."

◆　　◆　　◆

I WAS back in my seat. My sister was at my parents' table telling them something. The three of them kept looking at me and my mother put her hand to her face.

"Where were you?" Philip said.

"Staten Island," I said.

"You weren't missed."

My mother opened her purse and handed my

41

sister something. My sister left the dining room.

"Listen, Philip," I said.

"Yes."

"Suppose you knew something about someone."

"Suppose I knew what about whom?"

"Suppose you knew someone was a terrible person. Someone else you knew liked that person. You liked the person who liked the terrible person. You were afraid the terrible person would hurt the person you liked. Would you tell the person you liked that the other person was terrible?"

"I'd be inclined to tell," Philip said.

"You would?"

"But I might not."

"Why wouldn't you?"

"It's a complicated matter. I'd need to assess the consequences of telling as opposed to not telling. I'd consider the likelihood of the person I liked discovering for himself the shortcomings in the other. I'd question my own motives for telling or not telling. I'd weigh the competing claims of honesty and discretion."

"Philip," I said.

"Yes?"

"Pretend I never asked."

◆　　◆　　◆

MY SISTER came to see me. A moment before Tina had asked if I'd dance with her and I'd sent her away, asking if she'd forgotten what I'd said the last two times she asked.

"I hope you'll forgive me," my sister said, looking down at me in my seat.

"Forgive you for what?" I said.

"I've done something."

"What did you do?"

"You won't approve."

"Tell me. No, don't," I said, looking at Philip out of the corner of my eye. "Tell me somewhere else."

We left the table for a place by the wall.

"He's coming," my sister said.

"Who's coming?"

43

"My escort. I called him."

"Where is he coming?"

"Here."

"When?"

"Now. I told him to come."

"You didn't," I said.

"I'm afraid I did."

"You don't really mean it."

"I do."

"Oh, Carol."

"I couldn't help myself. I needed to see him. I can't deny my feelings. I hope you'll come to tolerate him someday. I know it won't be soon. It's so much to ask of you."

"It's all right, Carol," I said.

"Is it, Alex?"

"Yes. I mean, it's your life."

"Oh, thank you, Alex," my sister said. "I wished that you'd say that. Thank you so much, Alex."

◆　　　◆　　　◆

I RETURNED to my seat. Philip said something about all the intrigue but I ignored him.

"All this has nothing to do with the person you like and the terrible person, does it?" Philip said.

"No," I said.

No one but us was at the table. Everyone else was dancing or visiting someone or something. I had my elbow on the table and my chin in my hand.

"You seem forlorn," Philip said.

"Do I?" I said.

While he danced, Bob swung his jacket over his head.

"Isn't life complicated, Philip?" I said.

"Sometimes."

"Sometimes things get out of hand."

"They do."

"I mean, you lose control."

"I know."

I rested my chin in my other hand.

"Can I help?" Philip asked.

"No. No one can help."

I switched hands again and looked at Philip.

"Philip, are you being sympathetic and understanding?"

"I'm trying."

"That's nice of you, Philip."

"Thank you, Alex."

Bob let go of his jacket and it sailed across the dance floor.

"I'm sorry I wasn't friendly," I said.

"I'm sorry I was obnoxious," Philip said.

Bob took off his tie.

"Alex," Philip said.

"Yeah, Philip?"

"You haven't been nice to Tina."

"I know."

"I know something is on your mind."

"But that's no excuse, is it?"

"It really isn't."

"You're right, Philip. I'm going to do something about it."

◆　　◆　　◆

I FOUND Tina by herself, watching everyone dance.

"Hi," I said, walking up to her.

"Hi," she said.

"What do you think of this wedding?"

"It's good."

"Amanda looks pretty stunning, doesn't she?"

"Yes."

"You look nice yourself," I said.

"Thank you," Tina said, smiling.

"I like the bow in your hair."

"I chose it myself. I'm getting my ears pierced for my birthday."

"Do you—"

"What?"

"Do you want to dance or something?"

"Really?" Tina said with a bigger smile.

"I guess so. I never did it, though. I don't know how."

"Don't worry," Tina said. "I'll show you."

◆　　◆　　◆

WE WAITED three dances for a slow dance because that's what I wanted. Tina held my hand the whole time. My hand was sweating.

When the slow dance began, Tina led me onto the dance floor. She showed me how to put my arms around her, and then we were dancing, if you could call it that.

"How am I doing?" I said.

"Fine."

"Am I supposed to be leading?"

"Don't worry about that."

"You probably don't want me thinking about too much at once."

"I don't."

"I feel like everyone is looking at me. You should see me play baseball and basketball. I'm pretty coordinated."

Tina looked past me.

"Who's that man with Carol?"

"Where?" I stopped dancing and looked.

"There."

"I don't see them," I said, and started dancing

again. "I don't want to see them. It's probably Carol's escort."

"You're dancing better," Tina said. "You're not as stiff."

"I thought so, too."

"Why did Carol's escort come so late?"

"It's a long story."

"They're dancing now."

"Already?" I said.

"He's handsome."

"Do you think so? It's a matter of taste."

"You can tell they like each other. Her head is on his shoulder."

◆　　◆　　◆

I DANCED another dance with Tina and returned to my seat. I enjoyed dancing and would've danced some more if thinking about my sister dancing with Paine's cousin hadn't ruined it for me.

Philip told me that I'd done a good deed. Then

he said that my sister had come looking for me.

"A man was with her," he said.

"I know."

"Who is he?"

"Her escort."

"Why was he so late?"

"See, I have this friend, Alan Paine. We were walking to baseball practice one day. I told him—I don't want to get into it."

"He seemed nice," Philip said.

"My sister thinks so."

"You don't?"

"He lied to me. It wasn't about anything important, but he lied. Then he came to a baseball game—I don't want to get into that either."

"Your sister likes him," Philip said. "He likes her. You can tell."

◆　　◆　　◆

TINA RETURNED to the table. She said that my

sister and Willie were outside getting some fresh air and wanted to see me.

"Willie?" I said.

"Yes."

"You mean Leon."

"Who's Leon?"

"He's my sister's escort."

"He said his name was Willie."

"You heard wrong. It's Leon."

I was on my way from the dining room when Ida intercepted me.

"Oh, Alex. I want you to know how much I enjoyed watching you and Tina dance. It was lovely."

"Thanks."

"I enjoyed watching Carol dance, too. Willie seems a lovely boy."

◆　　　◆　　　◆

WILLIE SEEMS a lovely boy. That's what Ida said. She didn't say Leon seems a lovely boy. She said

Willie seems a lovely boy.

Tina said the boy with my sister had said that his name was Willie. Willie and Leon don't sound alike. Maybe Tina hadn't heard wrong.

What explained it, then? Why had Paine's cousin told Tina and Ida that his name was Willie?

Maybe he went by his middle name. Maybe Willie was a nickname.

Maybe he lied. Maybe he really *was* a pathological liar.

I reached the front of Maurice's Royal Manor and started down the steps. My sister was sitting at the bottom of the steps with Paine's cousin. She turned her head to see me and smiled. Then Paine's cousin turned his head to see me and smiled. But it wasn't Paine's cousin.

◆　　◆　　◆

I FROZE for a moment, then descended the rest of the steps.

"Willie—" I said.

"Hello, Alex."

"Willie, what are you doing here?"

"Sit down, Alex. You look dazed."

"Tell me what you're doing here, Willie," I said, sitting beside him.

"I'm Carol's escort," Willie said.

"No, you're not," I said.

"He is, Alex," my sister said.

"Paine's cousin is your escort," I said.

"No, he isn't," my sister said.

"He was supposed to be your escort," I said.

"No, he wasn't," my sister said.

"God, I'm confused," I said.

"Let's explain," Willie said.

"It's only merciful," my sister said.

They explained that they were attracted to each other the first time my sister came to a game. Willie called that night, and the next night they went to dinner together. The night after my sister came to the second game, they had dinner together again—I heard them come home that night and thought my sister was with Paine's cousin—and my sister surprised herself with her forwardness by asking Willie to escort her to the wedding.

My sister told my mother that Willie was going to escort her and my mother told me. She apparently didn't say Willie's name, though, and I assumed that Paine's cousin was going to be my sister's escort.

My mother told my sister that I seemed upset about it and my sister came to speak to me. I told her that Paine's cousin was a liar and cheater and insensitive without saying his name. My sister found it hard to believe about Willie—she thought I meant Willie—but called to tell him it would be better if he didn't escort her to the wedding.

When I told her I was sorry I ever told Paine it was all right for his cousin to call her, she became aware of the confusion. She called Willie to tell him what had happened and apologize, and since he lived a few blocks from Maurice's Royal Manor, he insisted on coming.

"Why did you wait to tell me?" I said.

My sister smiled.

"Yes, I could've told you sooner," she said. "But really, Alex. It was much more fun this way."

◆　　◆　　◆

BACK INSIDE my sister told my parents about the look on my face when I saw Willie. Everyone got a big laugh out of it. I said I was glad they were all amused and my mother asked where my sense of humor was.

Bob came and threw his arm around Willie. He welcomed him to Amanda's wedding and told him to enjoy himself and watch out for me because I couldn't be trusted.

My parents got up to dance. Bob began telling Willie about the restaurant supplies business. My sister asked if I'd dance with her because I looked so good dancing with Tina, and I said all right.

"Well?" she said when we were dancing.

"Well, what?"

"It's been quite an evening."

"It turned out all right," I said.

"I agree," my sister said.

"Look," I said. "Tina is dancing with Philip. Tina is nice. Philip is all right, too. You have to get to know him."

"I'm glad to hear you say that," my sister said.

"What do you think of my dancing?" I said.

"I'm impressed," my sister said.

"I don't even think Ida is so bad anymore," I said.

"You're gushing with benevolence," my sister said.

"I'm not that benevolent toward Paine's cousin. You didn't like him that much, did you?"

"Not that much."

"Why did you go out with him twice?"

"Don't you think that everyone is entitled to a second chance?"

"Maybe."

Philip and I bumped into each other.

"Sorry, Philip," I said.

"That's all right, Alex," he said.

"Did you ever read *Out of the Silent Planet?*" I asked my sister.

"No," she said.

"Philip recommended it. I'm going to take it out of the library. Willie is nice, isn't he, Carol?"

"Yes, Alex. Willie is nice."

"You like him, don't you?" I said.

"Yes, Alex," my sister said. "I like him."

◆　　◆　　◆

WILLIE AND my sister got married six months later. It was a small wedding in our apartment. The ceremony was in the living room.

When it was through, before everyone dispersed, my father said that he had something to say. He said that it was a joyous occasion and that he wished Willie and my sister a wonderful life because that was what they deserved.

Then he said that I had something to say. I had

arranged it with him beforehand.

I said that I had a poem by Ezra Pound to recite.
I had it memorized. Willie and my sister held hands
while I recited it.

> *Sing we for love and idleness,*
> *Naught else is worth the having.*
>
> *Though I have been in many a land,*
> *There is naught else in living.*
>
> *And I would rather have my sweet,*
> *Though rose leaves die of grieving,*
>
> *Than do high deeds in Hungary*
> *To pass all men's believing.*

At first no one said anything.

"Thank you, Alex," my sister finally said.

"You're welcome," I said.

"Thank you, Alex," Willie said.

"You're welcome," I said.

"That was lovely," Ida said.

"Come," my mother said. "Let's all go eat."

About the Author

Mark Geller is a sociologist and a writer, as well as a father, an avid watcher of sports, and a runner. A graduate of Queens College with a Ph.D. from Rutgers University, Mr. Geller lives in Highland Park, New Jersey, with his wife and two children. He is the author of MY LIFE IN THE SEVENTH GRADE, WHAT I HEARD, RAYMOND, and THE STRANGE CASE OF THE RELUCTANT PARTNERS.